KAY THOMPSON'S ELOISE

# Eloise Breaks Some Eggs

STORY BY **Margaret McNamara**

ILLUSTRATED BY **Tammie Lyon**

Ready-to-Read

Simon Spotlight

New York    London    Toronto    Sydney    New Delhi

SIMON SPOTLIGHT

An imprint of Simon & Schuster Children's Publishing Division
1230 Avenue of the Americas
New York, NY 10020
First Simon Spotlight hardcover edition January 2018
First Aladdin Paperbacks edition January 2005
SIMON SPOTLIGHT, READY-TO-READ, and colophon are
registered trademarks of Simon & Schuster, Inc.
For information about special discounts for bulk purchases, please contact Simon & Schuster
Special Sales at 1-866-506-1949 or business@simonandschuster.com.
The text of this book was set in Century Old Style.
Manufactured in the United States of America 1217 LAK
2 4 6 8 10 9 7 5 3 1
The Library of Congress has cataloged a previous edition as follows:
Library of Congress Cataloging-in-Publication Data
McNamara, Margaret.
Eloise breaks some eggs / written by Margaret McNamara ;
illustrated by Tammie Speer-Lyon.—1st ed.
p. cm. — (Kay Thompson's Eloise) (Ready-to-read)
Summary: Eloise's cooking lesson with Nanny and Cook is
disastrous—or would be, if Eloise could not order room service.
[1. Cookery—Fiction.]
I. Lyon, Tammie, ill. II. Title. III. Series. IV. Series: Ready-to-read.
PZ7.M47879343El 2005
[E]—dc22
2004008891
ISBN 978-1-4814-7680-5 (hc)
ISBN 978-0-689-87368-3 (pbk)

I am Eloise.
I am six.

I am a city child.
I live in a hotel
on the tippy-top floor.

This is Nanny.

She is my nanny.
My mother is mostly away.

"Eloise," says Nanny.
"It is time for your lesson."

I ask, "Piano?"
Nanny says, "No."

I ask, "French?"
Nanny says, "No."

I ask, "Poker?"
Nanny says, "No, no, no."

"It is time for
your cooking lesson.

# "Today you will cook eggs."

"I do not like to cook,"
I say.

"You like to break things,"
Nanny says.

"You break eggs
to cook them."

I say, "Let's go, go, go."

We take the elevator
to the kitchen.

I press every button.

"Today we will cook eggs,"
says the cook.

A bowl can make
a very good hat.
"No, no, no," says Nanny.

"Watch me," says the cook.
The cook is good.

"Now you try," he says.

I am very good.

"NO! NO! NO!" says Nanny.

"You broke the bowl!
You broke the plate!"
says the cook.

I say,
"I broke the eggs, too."

Nanny and
I take the elevator
to the tippy-top floor.
I press every button.

"You will never be a cook,"
says Nanny.
"How will you eat?"

I say, "Room service."
I pick up the phone.
I say, "It's me, Eloise.

"Two eggs,
  and charge it, please.
Thank you very much."